When Papa
Comes Home Tonight

When Papa Comes Home ◆ Tonight ◆

by Eileen Spinelli

ILLUSTRATED BY David McPhail

Simon & Schuster Books for Young Readers
New York   London   Toronto   Sydney

SIMON & SCHUSTER BOOKS FOR YOUNG READERS
An imprint of Simon & Schuster Children's Publishing Division
1230 Avenue of the Americas, New York, New York 10020
Text copyright © 2009 by Eileen Spinelli
Illustrations copyright © 2009 by David McPhail
SIMON & SCHUSTER BOOKS FOR YOUNG READERS is a trademark of Simon & Schuster, Inc.
The text for this book is set in Venetian.
The illustrations for this book are rendered in watercolor paint, pencil, and pen and ink.
Manufactured in China
2 4 6 8 10 9 7 5 3 1
Library of Congress Cataloging-in-Publication Data
Spinelli, Eileen.
When Papa comes home tonight / Eileen Spinelli;
illustrated by David McPhail.—1st ed.
p. cm.
Summary: A father and child enjoy a range of activities together before bedtime.
ISBN-13: 978-1-4169-1028-2 (hardcover)
ISBN-10: 1-4169-1028-X (hardcover)
[1. Stories in rhyme. 2. Father and child—Fiction.
3. Bedtime—Fiction.] I. McPhail, David, 1940– ill. II. Title.
PZ8.3.S759Whe 2009
[E]—dc22
2008008860

For Pete Pennock, Chuck Woods,
Rod Adams, and Bill Spinelli
—E. S.

For the big little guy, my grandson, Matthias
—D. M.

When Papa comes home tonight, dear child,
(I promise—not too late)
you'll hear me whistling up the road.
You'll meet me at the gate.

I'll lift you up. I'll swing you round.
And then we'll go inside.
You'll hand me fuzzy Teddy Bear.
You'll say: "Give him a ride!"

When Papa comes home tonight, dear child,
I'll let you help me cook.
We'll try that recipe for rice.
It's in the yellow book.

And when we wash the dishes,
you'll teach me that new song—
the one you learned a week ago.
I'll try to sing along.

When Papa comes home tonight, dear child,
we'll play bold knight and dragon.
Then later we'll collect my tools
and try to fix your wagon.

The stars will shine, the moon will splash
its light across the lawn.
We'll put on our pajamas.
I'll be the first to yawn.

I'll read your bedtime story.
Before it ends I'll doze.
You'll tap me on the shoulder.
I'll kiss you on the nose.

I'll give a hug to Teddy Bear.
You'll whisper in my ear:
"Don't let the bedbugs bite tonight.
I love you, Papa dear."

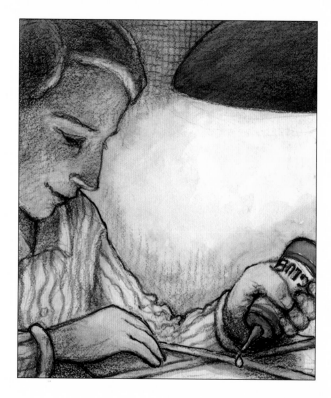

When you wake up tomorrow,
you'll find a brand-new kite.
I'll make it after you're asleep—

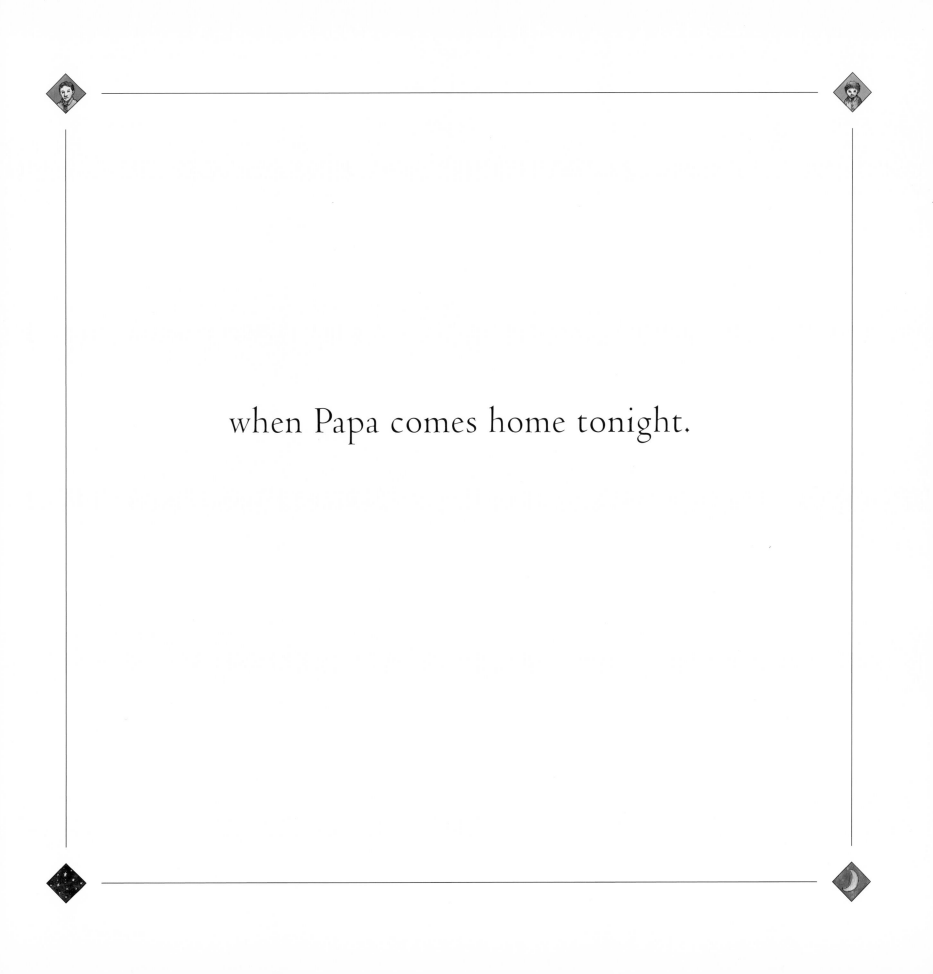

when Papa comes home tonight.